The KING'S EQUAL

by **KATHERINE PATERSON**

illustrated by **VLADIMIR VAGIN**

HarperCollins*Publishers*

Other books by Katherine Paterson

The Sign of the Crysanthemum
Of Nightingales That Weep
The Master Puppeteer
Bridge to Terabithia
The Great Gilly Hopkins
Angels and Other Strangers
Jacob Have I Loved
Consider the Lilies *(with John Paterson)*
The Smallest Cow in the World
(An I Can Read Book®)

The King's Equal
Text copyright © 1992 by Katherine Paterson
Illustrations copyright © 1992 by Vladimir Vagin
Printed in the U.S.A. All rights reserved.
1 2 3 4 5 6 7 8 9 10
First Edition

Library of Congress Cataloging-in-Publication Data
Paterson, Katherine.
  The king's equal / by Katherine Paterson ; illustrated by Vladimir
Vagin.
     p.   cm.
  Summary: In order to wear the crown of the kingdom, an arrogant
young prince must find an equal in his bride. Instead, he finds
someone far better than he.
  ISBN 0-06-022496-7. —ISBN 0-06-022497-5 (lib. bdg.)
  [1. Fairy tales.] I. Vagin, Vladimir Vasil'evich, date,   ill.
II. Title.
PZ8.P274Ki   1992   90-30527
[E]—dc20   CIP
                                                          AC

For my friends East and West
who have shared their passion for peace
especially
Stephanie Tolan
—K.P.

 any years ago in a country far away, an old king lay dying. Now the king was very wise and very good, and all the people loved him, so they were sad to know that he would soon leave them. But what made them even sadder was the knowledge that the king's son, Prince Raphael, would become their next ruler.

Prince Raphael was as rich and handsome as a prince should be. His father had assembled scholars from all over the world to teach him, so he was highly educated. The people should have been proud to have Raphael as their next king, but instead they were afraid.

"Look at his eyes," they said, "and see the arrogance of a man who admires only himself.

"Look at his mouth," they said, "and see the sneer of a man who thinks everyone else is stupid.

"Look at his hands," they said, "and see the grasp of a man who thinks everyone else's goods are his for the taking."

The old king, even while he was dying, understood the fears of his people. Just before the end, he called his son and all the councilors of the realm to come to his chamber.

"My son," he said, "with my last words, I want to give you my blessing."

"Well, of course," said Raphael, although he was far more interested in his father's lands and gold than he was in the good king's last words.

"You will become ruler when I die," the old king said, "for that is the ancient law that cannot be changed. But you will not wear my crown until the day you marry a woman who is your equal in beauty and intelligence and wealth."

The prince was angry at his father's words. "That is not a blessing!" he exclaimed. "That is a curse! Where shall I find a princess who is equal to me in every way?" Raphael demanded that the king take back this strange blessing. But the

king shook his head, and that very night he breathed his last breath and died.

Prince Raphael was so angry that he refused to mourn his father's death. When the councilors suggested that the flags be lowered and that the people be given time off from their work for the funeral, he was angrier still. "There will be plenty of time for holiday when I am crowned king," he said. "Tell the people to get back to work."

With heavy hearts the councilors announced there would be no period of mourning for the beloved old king. The only comfort they had was that Raphael might never be crowned. For where would such an arrogant man find a woman he would admit was his equal in every way?

⊢⊶ T W O ⊷⊣

At first Raphael was too busy to think about the crown. He had to have his portrait painted. In fact he had to have dozens of portraits painted to replace all the portraits of previous kings that hung in the palace and in museums and schoolhouses.

That gave him another idea. He would close the schools! Why should all those children be wasting their time trying to learn a dribble of geography here and a dabble of mathematics there? Wasn't he the most intelligent man in the known world? "Put the children to work!" he commanded. "From now on, I am doing the thinking for this country."

But the thing that took the most time and that Raphael enjoyed the most was collecting taxes. First he collected all the gold coins in the land. Then he collected all the silver. Next he sent out his agents to gather all the livestock and grain and vegetables. These he sold at an enormous profit to the people, who were forced to give him their last copper pennies to buy back their own meat and produce.

Raphael grew richer and richer, while the people grew poorer and poorer. "Ah," he said, looking into the mirror one day, "I have everything. Beauty, intelligence, and great, great wealth! I am the happiest man in the world."

Just then a voice whispered inside him, "You do not have *quite* everything. You do not wear your father's crown." And Raphael remembered to be angry.

That very day he sent for the councilors. "You lazy fools!" he said. "You heard my father's last words. Why have you not found me a wife?"

The councilors trembled from their wigs to their boot tips. What should they do? If they did not find the prince a wife, he would be angry. If they did find him a wife, would he believe her to be his equal?

"How can we find a woman who is equal to you, O Prince?" they asked. "You who are matchless in beauty and intelligence and wealth?"

"That is *your* problem," said Raphael. "And if you do not solve it by the end of the year, you shall be thrown into the dungeon until the flesh rots and falls from your bones."

The frightened councilors sent messengers over the lands and across the seas to search out the most beautiful princesses in the world. They brought them to the palace for Raphael to examine.

There was a princess whose hair was like spun sunlight falling across her shoulders and down to her waist.

There was a princess whose eyes were like lavender pools that sparkled in moonlight.

There was a princess with skin of alabaster on the body of a goddess.

The prince admired the hair of the first, the eyes of the second, and the body of the third, but he was not satisfied. "Faugh!" he shouted. "You can't reassemble princesses taking a bit of each! There is not a single creature here who could cast a shadow across my back, much less one who could stand beside me without shame. To the dungeon with you all!"

At these words the councilors trembled from their wigs to their boot tips. But the wisest councilor said, "If it please you, O Prince, there are still nine months before the year comes to a close. Besides, how can we search for your queen from the dungeon?"

Raphael was not pleased, but he had to keep his word. For according to the ancient law, the word of the ruler cannot be changed.

Once again the councilors sent messengers over the lands and across the seas. This time they were commanded to search out the most intelligent princesses in the world. They brought them to the palace for Raphael to examine.

There was a princess who could name the capital of every country in the world. "That is nothing," said Raphael. "She can't spell pterodactyl."

There was a princess who could multiply four-digit numbers in her head without using her fingers. "That is nothing," Raphael said. "She can't tell a

Tweedle-dum from a Tweedle-dee."

There was a princess who knew geography and mathematics and could recite the names and dates of every emperor of Byzantium for a thousand years. "That is nothing," said Raphael. "She doesn't know how to play backgammon. Besides, she has the face of a duck-billed platypus. To the dungeon with you all!"

Again the councilors trembled from their wigs to their boot tips, and again the wisest of them protested. "If it please you, O Prince, there are still six months left in the year," he said. "Besides, how can we search from the dungeon?"

The prince was not pleased, but he had to keep his word according to the ancient law.

This time the councilors were ill with anxiety. They sent out three times the number of messengers and found at last three princesses.

One was the daughter of a king who owned so much land that there was no one alive who knew how to measure the vastness of his domain. The second was the daughter of a king who owned a fleet of ships that sailed around the world bringing back fortunes each time they returned. The third was the daughter of a king who owned diamond mines. She was dressed in diamonds from head to toe. Each of her shoes was cut from a single perfect diamond.

At first Raphael seemed pleased. He had never seen so much wealth before. He

could not choose among the three princesses. "I shall marry all three," he said greedily.

But though the councilors trembled from their wigs to their boot tips, the bravest of them said, "You must choose one wife. There can only be one queen in our land, for that is the ancient law that cannot be changed."

Raphael became angry. "Then I will not marry any of these," he said. "They are stupid and ugly. To the dungeon, all of you, and take these useless girls with you."

The wisest councilor once more reminded Raphael of his word, for there were still three months left in the year. None of the councilors were cheered by this. They had searched the world over, and they were sure there was no one whom Prince Raphael would regard as his equal.

The councilors did not bother to send out any more messengers. Instead they began to put their affairs in order, for they knew that when the end of the year came, they would surely be cast into the dungeon until the flesh rotted and fell from their bones.

THREE

At that same time, in a far corner of the realm, there lived a poor farmer. His wife had died, leaving behind an only daughter. Rosamund (for that was the daughter's name) was cheerful and industrious and kind, and the farmer loved her more than his own life.

When the old king died, and Raphael began to rule, the farmer realized that what few things he had would soon be taken by the greedy prince. The farmer had only one old nanny goat, but that spring she had twin kids. So the farmer gathered all the bread he had in the house and told Rosamund to take the goats and go to a pasture far away in the mountains.

Rosamund did not want to leave her father. "Please come with me," she begged him.

"I must stay," he said, "and try to harvest our grain. There is a chance that Raphael's agents will not find our tiny farm in this far corner of the realm."

"Then let me stay," Rosamund begged. "Isn't it better to share hunger with one you love than to feast alone?"

"No, my child," he said. "You must go, for I promised your dying mother to take care of you. If the agents should come, at least you and the goats will be saved."

With a heavy heart, Rosamund left her father and took the goats to the mountain pasture. At first she was sick with loneliness, but it was not in Rosamund's nature to give in to despair. As the days went by, she began to make a cheerful home for herself and the goats in the old goatherd's shack.

The mountains were beautiful in the summer. She loved to frolic in the meadow with the goats, and often she would sing to them. There was plenty of sweet grass for the goats to eat. There were roots and berries and wild grain. Rosamund drank the milk of the nanny goat and made cheese and bread.

However, winter comes early in the mountains. With the first snows, food became scarce. Rosamund had dried some grass, but that soon ran out, so the girl shared her tiny store of grain with her animals. Still, as the nanny had less to eat, she had less milk to give.

One day, as the goats were rooting about in the snow hoping to find something to fill their empty bellies, and Rosamund was shivering inside the shack trying to decide whether or not to use the last of her store of grain to make bread, she heard a shriek of fear.

Rosamund grabbed her staff and dashed outside. The nanny goat was bleating in alarm, for there in the snow stood a giant wolf with one of her babies in his powerful jaws.

"How dare you attack my friend!"

Rosamund cried.

The wolf let go of the kid as gently as a mother cat drops a kitten, and he looked up at Rosamund with such sad and hungry eyes that she could only feel sorry for him. "Poor thing," she said. "Come into the shack with us. Isn't it better for us to share the last that we have and die as friends than to tear each other apart and die as enemies?"

"You are a kind girl," the wolf said, his voice rumbling like distant thunder, "and I promise you that your kindness will not go unrewarded."

"Who are you?" Rosamund asked, for she had never met a wolf who could speak.

"I am the Wolf," he answered, "and I will prove myself your friend."

Rosamund, the goats, and the wolf went into the shack, where Rosamund took the last of the grain and divided it. She gave a portion to each of the goats, and the last two portions she ground into flour with which she made a little loaf of bread. This she broke in half and shared with the wolf.

"Now I will sing all the songs that I know," she said. "Isn't it better for us to end our lives with a song on our lips than to die in sorrow?"

"You are a wise girl," the wolf said. "Such wisdom will not go unrewarded."

Later that night one of the kids bleated with hunger. "I'm sorry, little friend," Rosamund said. "But the grain jar is empty. I have nothing more to give you."

"Are you sure?" asked the wolf.

To show him, Rosamund raised the lid of the jar, and there she saw a handful of grain.

"How could it be?" she wondered, but, gratefully, she divided the grain into portions as before.

From that time on, each time she thought the jar had been emptied, the wolf asked, "Are you sure?" and each time Rosamund raised the lid, there was a handful of grain to be divided among the friends.

In this way they lived happily together for many weeks. Still, Rosamund worried about her father and wondered if he was well.

"Why do you look sad, my friend?" the wolf asked her one night.

"I am anxious about my father," Rosamund said.

"Your father is well," said the wolf. And because Rosamund knew that he was not an ordinary wolf, she believed what he said and was comforted.

"I am also anxious for my country," she said. "It is ruled by a greedy and arrogant prince who cares nothing for the welfare of the people."

"Ah," said the wolf. "That is the kingdom that has searched in vain for a young woman of wealth and intelligence and beauty. If such a one were to appear, the country might be saved." He turned his great solemn eyes on Rosamund. "Would you like to help your people?" the wolf asked.

"If only I could," Rosamund answered. "But as you can see, I am neither very beautiful nor very clever, and I am so poor I would have starved and my goats with me if you had not come to our aid."

"Look at my neck," the wolf said.

Rosamund looked, and for the first time noticed that the wolf wore around his furry neck a thin circlet of gold.

"Take my collar and put it upon your head," the wolf said, "and go down to the capital city. You will find there a wise councilor who serves the prince. Tell him that you are the princess he has been searching for."

Rosamund laughed out loud. "I am no princess. You of all creatures should know that."

But the wolf did not laugh. "On the night that you were born, your mother lay dying. With her last words, she gave you a blessing. She said that you were to be a king's equal."

Rosamund grew solemn. The idea of going to the capital and making such an extravagant claim frightened her. But she thought of her dead mother and her loving father and all the people who were suffering, and determined to make the journey.

She took the wolf's circlet of gold from around his neck and placed it upon her head. Suddenly, the tiny shack was filled with light.

"Is it magic?" she asked.

"The circlet of a friend is always magic,"

the wolf answered. "Now go," he said.

"I will never forget you," Rosamund said.

"Nor I you," replied the wolf. "Yet, when you go into the world of people, do not say that you have met me. They will not understand our friendship."

Thus it was that Rosamund kissed the goats, bowed solemnly to her friend the wolf, and made her way down the winter mountain to the capital.

❯━━❳ F O U R ❲━━❮

he last day of the year had arrived. The councilors who had lived the past twelve months in fear were now resigned to their fate. They spent the final hours with their families, comforting their weeping wives and embracing their sad-faced children.

At an hour before midnight, the wisest of the councilors rose from the family table, bathed, and dressed himself in the finest robes that he owned. Just as he was about to leave for the palace, there came a knock on the door. The councilor opened the door, and there before him stood the most beautiful young woman he had ever seen.

"I have been sent to your house," she said, "for you are to take me to the prince."

The councilor hardly dared to hope, and yet ... "I must warn you," he said, "the prince is a very hard man. If he does not accept you as his equal, I cannot promise that any of us will escape with our lives."

"I am not afraid," Rosamund answered. "Neither should you be, for I promise you that tonight you will sleep in your own bed."

The councilor did not question further, for, he thought, if this young woman were half as wise or wealthy as she was beautiful, no man would be able to resist her.

When they arrived at the palace, the prince was already shouting. "Where is my wife, you incompetent fools? The year is over and still you have not found her! To the dungeon, all of you!"

The wise councilor stepped forward. "Your majesty," he said, bowing deeply, "may I present the Princess Rosamund."

On the first stroke of midnight there came before the throne the most beautiful woman the prince had ever seen. From the first moment he saw her, Raphael was determined to have Rosamund for his wife.

"You are the most beautiful creature I have ever seen," he said.

"If you say so, my lord," Rosamund said humbly.

Suddenly the prince remembered his father's words. The queen must be the king's equal in intelligence and wealth as well as beauty.

"You are certainly beautiful," Raphael said, "but are you intelligent? As intelligent as I?"

"That is for you to decide," Rosamund said. "But I do know one thing that no one else knows."

"What could you know that I do not?" the prince asked haughtily.

"I know," said Rosamund quietly, so that only he could hear, "I know that you are very lonely."

The prince looked at her in astonishment. Until that moment, he had not known how very lonely he was. How could this woman, who was after all a stranger, know him better than he knew himself?

"Very well," he said gruffly, "you have passed two tests, but there is still the requirement of wealth. What proof do you offer that your wealth can equal mine?"

"None, my lord, for as you see, I have brought nothing with me. But perhaps there is a way we can judge. Is there at this moment anything you desire that you do not have?"

When he heard her question, the prince's brain whirled with thoughts of vast lands, and sailing ships, and diamonds, and above all, his father's crown. "Of course," he said angrily, "there are things I desire that I do not possess."

"Then," said Rosamund quietly, "perhaps you are poorer than I, for there is nothing I desire that I do not already possess."

"The King's Equal!" shouted the wisest of the councilors. "She is found!" And all the councilors shouted: "Hooray for the King's Equal!"

Raphael was pleased, for at that moment the thing he desired most was for Rosamund to be his wife. He held out his hand to her. "It is decided," he said. "According to the ancient law and my father's blessing, you shall be queen of the realm and my wife."

But Rosamund did not take his hand. "I shall be glad to be queen of the realm," she said, "but I'm afraid I cannot be your wife, because by your own admission you have declared that I am the most beautiful creature you have ever seen, that I have knowledge you do not possess, and that although I have everything I desire, there are many things you desire that are not yours. By your own words, my lord, you have declared me *more* than equal to you."

Raphael was furious, but he knew that his own foolishness had been his undoing. Now that she seemed unattainable, he desired her more than ever.

"What must I do, then, to win you for my wife?" he cried out.

"I am not sure," said Rosamund, "but perhaps there is a way. Up in a mountain pasture there is an old goatherd's shack and three goats. You must go and live there and take care of the goats for one year. At the end of the year you must return to the palace, bringing all three goats with you alive and well. If in that time you have become in every way my equal, then you and I will be married and rule the realm together as king and queen."

Thus it was that Rosamund sent for her father to live with her in the palace while Raphael set out for the mountain to live a year with the goats.

osamund hardly let Raphael out of sight before she went to work. She put aside her circlet of gold, rolled up her sleeves, and set about undoing all the evil that Raphael had managed to do in his short reign. The realm had never known such a cheerful, industrious, and kind ruler. It was a year of good weather and bountiful crops. The children returned to school, and everyone had plenty and to spare.

In the meantime Raphael had reached

the mountain pasture. The old goat and her two kids greeted him with joyful bleats, which turned to mournful wails when they realized Raphael had brought them nothing to eat.

Moreover, they smelled, as goats tend to, so Raphael kicked them out of the shack into the cold, where they stood outside the door calling out even more piteously. The prince ignored their cries as he searched the shack for something to put in his own empty stomach.

At last he found the grain jar, and because he didn't know how to grind wheat into flour to bake bread, he began to chew on the hard grains.

Suddenly he heard a shriek from the snowy pasture. It sounded as though one creature were being killed by another. Raphael was terrified. Suppose some ferocious beast were to attack him on this forsaken mountain? No one would hear his cries for help. He cursed Rosamund for sending him to this wild place. But then, remembering that he must bring back all three goats alive and well to the palace at the end of the year, he grabbed a staff and rushed out of the shack.

There in the snow stood a large wolf with one of the small goats in his powerful jaws. "Stop!" Raphael shouted, waving the staff. "That's my goat. Leave it alone and get out of here."

The wolf let go of the kid as gently as a mother cat drops a kitten. "I didn't know this goat was yours," he said.

Now Raphael had never heard any animal, much less a wild beast, speak before, and he trembled from his wig to his boot tips. "Wh-wh-wh-who are you?" he asked the wolf.

"I am a friend of Rosamund's," said the wolf. "That is all you need to know."

"Then why are you stealing her goat?" asked Raphael, feeling a bit braver.

"I wasn't stealing her goat. We're friends, too, the goats and I. We live together in this shack. I'd just gone out for the day, and when I came back, I found my friends shivering in the snow with nothing to eat and a stranger in our home gobbling up all our grain. We played a rather simple trick to rid ourselves of an unwanted intruder. It seems to have worked."

"Rosamund never mentioned you to me," said Raphael grumpily.

"No," said the wolf, "she wouldn't have." He turned to the goats. "Now that the foolish knave is out of the shack," he said, "let's go inside and see if he's left us anything to eat."

The wolf followed the goats inside and shut the door. At first Raphael was too proud to knock at the door and beg the animals' forgiveness. As day turned into night and the wind came up and howled across the mountain pasture, Raphael could no longer afford pride—he had to humble himself or freeze to death.

"Please, sir," he begged, "it's terribly cold out here. I may even freeze to death. May I come in?"

"Of course you may come in," said the wolf. "Actually, we need your help. Paws and hooves are no good for making fires and grinding flour and baking bread."

"I'm sorry," Raphael said. "I don't know how to make a fire or grind flour or bake bread."

"Oh well, never mind," said the wolf. "Just do what I tell you, and we'll manage."

That is how things went for Raphael. The wolf taught him all the things Rosamund had known how to do—to make a fire, to grind flour, to bake bread. And when spring and summer came— to gather roots and berries and wild grain, and to dry grass for the coming winter.

As the months went by, Raphael's skin

burned and his hands grew callused. His fancy clothes were in tatters, and mischievous birds stole his wig for a nest.

The young goats taught him how to dance, and around the fire at night, the wolf taught him all the songs that Rosamund used to sing and told him tales of ancient times.

⇥ ≼ S I X ≽ ⇤

n one such night, Raphael looked at the wolf's strong eyes, bright with firelight, and whispered a question: "Who are you?"

"I am the Wolf," the great beast answered. "And someday I shall prove to be your friend."

For the first time in his life Raphael was happy, for he had friends.

Yet never a day went by when he didn't think of Rosamund—the rich, the wise, the beautiful Rosamund—and long to have her for his wife.

At last the time came when the days grew cold and short and snow lay once more upon the ground. "It is time," said the wolf one night, "time for you and the goats to go down to the palace."

Raphael trembled when he heard these words, for as much as he longed to see Rosamund, he was afraid to face her. What would she think of him? Then he remembered that the wise wolf who had taught him everything was her friend as well.

"Come with us, my friend," Raphael begged the wolf.

The wolf shook his head. "I belong to these mountains," he said. "But give my love to the beautiful Rosamund, remind her of her mother's blessing, and tell her that her wisdom and kindness have not gone unrewarded."

On the last day of the year, Raphael made his way down the winter mountain and entered the gates of the palace followed by three thin goats.

He knew that he looked like a goatherd, so he did not present himself at the great front door but went around to the kitchen. Inside he could hear a woman singing one of the songs the wolf had taught him. He listened for a few minutes, gathering his courage. Then he pushed open the heavy door.

Rosamund was standing before the stove, her sleeves rolled up, her face pink from the heat.

"Ah, Raphael!" she exclaimed. "Has a year gone by so quickly?"

"I've brought your goats," Raphael said.

"Yes," Rosamund said, thinking of the magical night when she had first met Raphael. Suddenly, she put her hands on her hair. "Oh," she said, "I forgot my circlet."

"You are even more beautiful than I remembered," he said softly.

Rosamund laughed. "No," she said. "Not really. But perhaps *you* have changed."

"Yes," said Raphael. "The mountain has changed me. I found friends there."

"A man who has friends is truly rich," Rosamund said in a voice so low he did not hear.

"I have learned much from my friends," Raphael continued. "I have learned to sing and play and make my daily bread. I have also learned that I am not as handsome or clever or wealthy as I once thought. Indeed, my gracious lady, I have nothing to offer you but these three goats, and they are yours already."

Sadly, Raphael turned to leave. "I almost forgot," he said. "The wolf sends you his love."

"Wait," she said, holding out her hand. "Don't go."

That very night Raphael and Rosamund were married and crowned king and queen, and they, and all in the land, lived happily together for many, many years.

But every winter, just at the turning of the year, the king and queen, and their children after them, went up into the far mountains, where it was said that they visited an old friend.

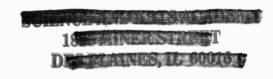